HERO BEGINNINGS

HERO BEGINNINGS

Troy Malin
Vlad A. Malin
Zimry Osburn
Jade Malin
Daniel De La Torriente

Monkey's Big Book

CONTENTS

Introduction	1
Trials and Tribulations	2
A Tale of a Hyblaen	6
A Reaper's Legacy	9
Twangs and Flashes	17
The Case of the Missing Gold	51
Ravens' Rise and Falcons' Fall	57
Maktuf: The Origin Story	61
Epilogue	64

Copyright © 2024 by Monkey's Big Book

All rights reserved. No part of this book may be reproduced in any manner whatsoever without written permission except in the case of brief quotations embodied in critical articles and reviews.

First Printing, 2024

Introduction

Hero Beginnings is a collection of backstories describing specific characters, which take place within a time of turmoil and strife in the Nexar Galaxy. As part of the galaxy sees a glimpse of hope for freedom from the tyrannical empire of Purple-Hood in the form of a New Government, many agents of tyranny continue to work in secret. In a time of struggle and lawlessness, the environment is right for leaders to step up and heroes to emerge. Each story focuses on a single character, but they all end with a connection to the greater story. We hope you enjoy the intricate worlds and characters of *Hero Beginnings*, and remember that these tales are only the beginnings.

Trials and Tribulations

BY TROY MALIN

Danny Bighat's father, Johnathan Bighat, was dead, and all Danny had to remember him by was his big hat, which he always wore. Apparently, it was a part of family history, but this was the least of Danny's worries. Right now, he had to run away, far away, so Purple-Hood and his henchmen did not capture him, as had happened to his father. He was not alone. His friend, Rustler Red, was the son of James Red, who had been friends with Danny's father. There were also his pals, Randy Lance and Thomas Mech. These four were now on the run from Purple-Hood, the supreme leader and the usurper of the galaxy, who wanted to exterminate anyone who posed a threat of overthrowing him. This included Danny and his friends.

"Watch out for that one!" said Randy, as he whacked one of Purple-Hood's henchmen with his lance.

"Thanks," said Danny, "I wish my father had passed down to me a fancy weapon instead of this hat, but I do think my hat is still enjoyable." They were now running in and out of buildings. Purple-Hood's henchmen were close behind them.

"We need to find some way out of this," said Rustler Red.

"I know," said Danny. "Up ahead, there is a spaceport. Let's catch a ride out of here." There was a spaceport up ahead, but as they reached it, they saw a battalion of Purple-Hood's henchmen awaiting them.

"Of course," thought Danny. "They shut down all spaceports to keep anyone from escaping."

However, there was one ship that was between them and the henchmen. It was obviously not part of the spaceport, for it was parked outside. The spaceship was blue and white. It had four engines with two wings that extended out in front of the hull. The name Agilis was painted on her side.

"To that ship," cried Danny! "It is our only chance of getting out of here." It would be close, for the henchmen had just spotted them. They charged at Danny and his friends; weapons bared. Just then the ship was activated. Then it took off.

"Wait for us," cried Danny! "Don't leave us behind to be captured!" The ship reared round and fired upon Purple-Hood's henchmen. They scattered in all directions.

"This is our chance!" exclaimed Danny. Rustler Red blasted off toward the ship on his jet pack.

"Hey, no fair!" said Randy. "We don't have jet packs." Rustler Red had reached the ship. He pointed down to his friends. Then the ship flew down to them, and the doors opened.

"In we go," said Thomas Mech. They all got on. The ship blasted away, but three of Purple-Hood's starships were after them. They opened fire on the Agilis.

"They are trying to shoot us down!" said Danny. The Agilis skillfully maneuvered around the laser bolts, reared round and shot down one of the starships. Then it flew right at the other two starships. They moved out of the way and continued firing. When the Agilis was between the two enemy starships, its wings suddenly folded back with such force that they karate chopped both of the enemy starships in half. Then the Agilis flew off. Danny and his friends were saved by this mysterious pilot and his ship.

"Well, that's one good pilot," said Danny.

"I have never seen anything like it," agreed Randy. "Speaking of which, here he is now." The pilot had come down into the room. He wore a blue outfit. A pair of ocular enhancers hung at his side, and he wore a white combat helmet.

"Hello friends," said he. "My name is Marcus Torrent."

"We are very much obliged to you," said Danny. "If it weren't for you, we would have been captured."

"My pleasure," said Marcus. "I will do whatever I can to hinder Purple-Hood."

"You're the best pilot I have ever seen," said Randy. "I have never seen anyone do the things I saw you do."

"I have been on the run for some time now," said Marcus. "One needs these skills to survive. I am what you call a top-notch pilot. Now if you will excuse me, I have to put the coordinates for the next mining facility into the navigation computer. I need to pick up some supplies." It was a pleasant trip, and Marcus Torrent told them how he was the only one who was able to escape Purple-Hood.

"My Brother John Torrent didn't make it, but before he was killed by Purple-Hood, he gave me a strange list of numbers that didn't make any sense. He told me not to reveal the to anyone, even if it was to come to death. I stole myself a ship, and now have been on the run ever since.

"Well, that's just weird," said Danny. "Because my father also gave me a strange list of numbers, right before he was executed."

"How interesting," said Randy. At last, they arrived at the mining facility. It was mainly meant for gold mining, but there were some other metals mined also, like tin and lead.

"Follow me," said Marcus. "Stay close. Don't let too many people see you. Trouble is always brooding in places like this." They walked up to a supply stand. Marcus was about to make his order when a gun sounded and some of Purple-Hood's henchmen appeared.

"These men are wanted for high treason against his majesty Purple-Hood," said one. "They must be terminated at once."

"How did they find us," wondered Danny?

"There are henchmen stationed all across the galaxy," said Marcus. "They must have been notified by the last bunch we came across. Come, let's get out of here!" They ran back to the Agilis. Marcus got in first. He ran into the cockpit and fired up the engines. Then came Rustler Red, then Randy Lance, then Thomas Mech and last of all Danny Bighat.

Danny was about to jump on board, when he was grabbed from behind and shoved down. Then the Agilis took off.

"We have to go back for Danny," cried Thomas Mech. "We can't leave him to die!" But it was too late. Danny was surrounded.

"I can't get him," said Marcus. "If I fire my guns, Danny and the henchmen will die. If we go back, we will be captured. We have no choice. We must fly." Everyone saw the sense in this. So, it was with great sorrow that Danny's three friends consented. Meanwhile, Danny was surrounded and it looked like it was all up with him. When all of a sudden, the leader of the henchmen said,

"Stop, we have new orders. We are not to harm this man. His majesty Purple-Hood says he has made a deal with Magnesia Starbrand, leader of the underground resistance. They have decided to split the galaxy between them. This planet is no longer under our jurisdiction. We will depart from here." And to Danny's utter amazement, the henchmen left. What was the meaning of this?

"Hey partner, are you looking for a mining buddy," said a miner? "I just got here and I don't know anyone. When I saw you, my heart went out to you, and I decided I wanted to be with you." Danny saw no reason to object. His friends had all gone and there was nothing for him to do anyway.

"All right, let's get to it," said Danny.

"Thank you," said the miner. "By the way, my name is Jerry, Jerry Wilkans."

'Thank you, Jerry," said Danny. "Now come on, let's go get some tools and stake a claim."

A Tale of a Hyblaen

BY JADE MALIN

My name is Harpo, and as you might guess I am from Hybla. My people are known as Hyblaens. I have a baby brother named Remo, but we were never like the other Hyblaens. We never thought it was right to rob and scrap ships like the other Hyblaens, and we felt left out. I also always wanted to be a police officer, and my brother always wanted to be a mechanic. That is very strange for Hyblaens.

Unfortunately, my parents were very old and could no longer take care of us. The problem was we were too young to take care of ourselves, so we had to be put up for adoption. Now you might expect us to be adopted by someone from Hybla, but that is where you are wrong. Every Hyblaen heard about our strange dislike for robbing and scrapping ships. So unfortunately, no one really wanted to adopt us.

Well, that was until one day we were adopted by a Police Chief, and my dream of becoming a police officer came true. We now have a human brother named Junior. My new dad's name is Sheriff, and my new mom's name is Sophie.

And now I can fast forward around nine years later. I am 21 and Remo is 17. Because I am grown up, everyone calls me Police Officer Harpo. Oh, and Remo. is now a mechanic. But he was still called Remo. You might think that the other police officers were suspicious of Remo and I scrapping the police station, but they knew we meant no harm.

One day I was looking out the window when I saw a starship. This starship looked very suspicious for some reason. I was about to tell my dad, when it dropped a large, round, black sphere. Then I knew instantly, it was a bomb! I tried to run to the nearest exit! But, when the bomb hit, I thought it was the end! I dove under a table when it hit. Somehow I lived and escaped with only a few scratches. But then I saw a purple hooded guy, and even worse, my dad laying on the ground. I went to him. In his last words he told me some measurements and mixes of chemicals. He said they were very important. This meant I had to value my life even more, because I was the only one who knew the formula. I did not have much time to think. I jumped into my small flying police car and flew off! But, as I did one of the starships shot my engine, and my police car crashed. When I came to, I realized I was in a bush surrounded by strange figures. One of them spoke up and said, "We are the Scavengers." I told them my name is Harpo, Police Officer Harpo. I told them what happened, and they were about to speak, but then we heard something in the bushes.

Emmit, one of my fellow police officers, hopped out of the bushes. Then some more officers came behind him. I saw both of my brothers and my mother had survived! My mother said, "You are the new Police Chief, because your father died, and you are his eldest son". I told her my first move would be to build a new police station. Oh, then I asked the Scavengers, "Would you like to join the Police force?" They agreed.

I told Remo to try to fix what he could of the wreckage. He ran off into the forest with his tool box. Then I sent some other police officers to recover what wreckage they could. Some other policemen started looking for food, wood and leaves for shelter and a fire.

Eight years passed and the police station was finally complete. By then Purple-Hood had changed. He split half of the galaxy with Magnesia Starbrand. She and I have been working undercover together for a very long time to overthrow Purple-Hood, and that is how I knew she would be great at ruling. In fact, she ruled over the half that I lived on.

Unfortunately, an evil rebel force had rallied up and was trying to overthrow Magnesia Starbrand. I was not going to let that happen, so I decided to join her army. I contacted her and she agreed. So, I met with her and she appointed me as a General in her army, so now my formal name is General Harpo.

And that is my story.

A Reaper's Legacy

BY DANIEL DE LA TORRIENTE

In a universe called the Reaper Dimention there is a planet known as Umbra in a galaxy called the Twilight System, where no intelligent beings like humans live. It is full of normal wildlife and greenery. One thousand years before the events of this story, a group of old and mysterious scientists traveled to Umbra to experiment on creatures known as raptors. They were aggressive dinosaurs that proved to be excellent hunters and fighters. The scientists attempted to cross-breed raptors with humans, using their Electromagnetic Breeding Tank (EMBT), to create a figure with enhanced senses and superior intelligence. They just had one minor problem... there were no other humans on the planet. These scientists were the first to set foot there. They struggled to find a solution until...

"We don't have any other options," said one scientist.

"It's too dangerous. We can't be sure what will happen," said another.

"What will happen to us?" said a third.

"We should at least try," put in another.

"Everyone, " said the last scientist, "we have just done something that will make history. Using our invention, the Versible Portal, we have the ability to travel across dimensions! But, we are old in age. We can't live forever. What better way is there to go down in history then to complete this ultimate experiment?!"

These scientists did go down in history, but not in the way they expected. They bred themselves with the raptors to create the ultimate humans. But, when the process was almost complete the EMBT mysteriously imploded on itself, sending a shockwave all the way around the planet wiping out animals and plants alike and destroying the Versible Portal. Not only did the planet change, but so did the scientists. They did not remain human, they created something else; something much stronger, much faster, and much more deadly. It was something that no other combination of creatures could ever form. They changed into what became to be known as, Reapers.

When these Reapers were formed by the EMBT, the scientists, if you could still call them that, strangely became younger than they were before. They could still communicate with each other, but not in normal English. Instead, it sounded like a growl of some kind, like a mixture of a wolf and a bear. They also looked strange. They had a human frame, but with muscles much more prominent. They had retractable claws as long as a bear's, but with feet shaped more like a tiger's. They had what looked like the head of a wolf, but it was black and shadowy and almost fading in and out of reality. Their skin was plated with hardened scales that made them look like impenetrable reptiles. They had green eyes that looked like they were dueling flames in the heads of the creatures.

The Reaper population grew immensely, and they eventually taught themselves how to talk in a form of English by reading the lab reports and books the scientists had left behind. They aged slowly, potentially allowing them to live hundreds of years. They built massive cities using their stunning intellect, and they flourished.

About seven hundred years ago, a Reaper named Chronos, King of The Under, conquered Umbra and met one of the Reapers, whose name was Issa. They became fast friends and eventually they were married. They had two sons, Ravendor and Azrail. The pair grew up in Umbra. They were completely different from one another. Azrail, who was the older brother, was clingy and very wild, while Ravendor was independent and very relaxed most of the time. When they were older, Azrail was very mischievous, and he and his brother would fight all the time. Though the reason is still unknown, Azrail was always getting into trouble. He got into so much trouble that his mother and father said that if he didn't stop his rebelliousness, they would have no choice but to exile him from Umbra.

One day, Azrail was playing hide-n-seek with Ravendor, and he chose his father's room for his hiding spot. Chronos had a very expensive item on his shelf. It was a very beautiful, but fragile, katana which was handcrafted by the first generation of Reapers hundreds of years before. Azrail was not being careful and he bumped into the shelf, knocking the katana to the floor. Ravendor, Chronos, and Issa rushed into the room to find it shattered, and most of the shards had pierced Azrail. That was the last straw. For everyone's safety, they had to exile him.

Azrail had almost died, and what would his parents do if Ravendor had been in that room with him and they both were seriously injured? He had to leave. But he was just a boy, and by Reaper creed, no one that is juvenile can leave until full growth. So, when they were old enough, they parted ways. Azrail left the planet Umbra, full of rage. Rage not aimed at his parents, but at himself. He loved his family very much, and they loved him, but his tendency to get into trouble was too risky to have him around. Putting him in confinement would be far worse. Azrail knew they were doing what was best.

Around three hundred years had passed and Ravendor met a female Reaper named Amria. They fell in love and were married two years later. Then, one hundred and ten years later, I was born.

My name is Titan. My father's name was Ravendor. My mother's name was Amria. I am the youngest of six children. My brothers' names are: Acidious the Fang, Ingressous the Hammer, Spike the Scythe, Forum the Hunter, and Sunflash the Axe. Reapers give their children unique titles in hopes that one day they will create or serve a nation united under it. Though I do not know why I never received a title, my mother always told me that I was destined to find my own. I was not weighed down by the pressure of uniting a nation under some weapon. I suppose you're wondering why I'm speaking of my mother and father in the past tense. Well, I guess I will have to tell you, won't I?

You see, my father and uncle had an "incident". After Azrail was exiled, Chronos' wife, Issa, became seriously ill. Sadly, medicine is not a skill in which Reapers excel. Issa died two weeks after she had become ill. Chronos left Umbra heart-broken and returned to The Under, leaving Umbra in the hands of his son. Ravendor vowed to his father to keep his home planet just and pure, though his vow would come back to bite him many years later. When my brothers and I were born, we grew up together and got along much better than my father and uncle had. We lived on the edge of a dense jungle forest surrounded by high walls.

At the time of the "incident," Acidious was one hundred and ten, which is still pretty young. Ingressous was ninety, Spike was seventy, and Forum was fifty. Sunflash was thirty, and I was ten, which is practically an infant. What happened to my father changed and scarred my life in so many ways. It was all our birthdays, because we were all born on the same day but twenty years apart. My father was about to cut the giant chocolate cake the local Reaper citizens had made. All Reapers also eat a lot, not just teenage boys. We heard a loud boom outside our massive, kingly palace. It sounded like the loudest earthquake or the biggest wave you have ever heard. It sounded like the whole planet sensed an immense evil on its ground and wished it to leave, but the shaking we felt was not Umbra repelling an evil. It was an evil. Azrail, my uncle, had returned from exile, and he had brought an entire army with him. They were shooting rockets and bombs off of their ships while their ground troops landed. They caught us by complete surprise, so that our own forces had no time to assemble. My mother was scared for all our safety.

"Ravendor, what are we going to do if Azrail really wants you dead?" She knew that Azrail was not interested in friendly terms, and that he would not rest until Ravendor was killed or a prisoner for torture. Ravendor reached for Amria and hugged her tightly. When they parted, he had both hands on her shoulders and looked her in the eyes.

"Amria, we both know he will not stop until I am dead or in a cell on his ship. Gather the children and go to the Versible Portal. Do you still remember where it is?" Our city had rebuilt the Versible Portal after my eighth birthday.

Amria wiped a tear away from her eye. She nodded, "Yes." Ravendor guided her to where the six children were huddled together, scared for our lives. "Children, pack everything you can. We're leaving." She said this holding her composure very well in front of us. Forum, the keenest of us, noticed our father leaving. We all did, but something told him this was not right.

"Mama, where's father going," he asked, staring at his mother's green eyes. All Reapers have green eyes, but Amria's were the most notable of our family.

"Your father is going to take care of some business dear," she said while wiping a tear away, hoping Forum had not noticed. He did and using his wits he helped his mother guide his siblings towards the forest. They already had their things packed, and my mother carried me since letting me walk would slow us down. I was facing away from the jungle and towards the chaos that ensued before me. Some of the younger and quicker Reapers managed to escape. But, the elderly could not move as fast, so most of the adults chose to stay and protect them. Now, I have to say that Reapers normally never lose fights. Even if it is a small army, only two or three Reapers are all that's needed to defeat them, but if you have hundreds of well-equipped and well-trained soldiers firing down on them, it is not even a fair fight. The Reapers were wiped out by the foreign soldiers in seconds. My father was the only other Reaper still alive and only because Azrail wanted him alive. We did not want to leave him, so we hid in some dense trees and listened. This is most of what we heard.

"Hello again Azrail!" My father shouted across the field. He had a flaming blade in each hand, which look like two katanas, only much more durable, and they were on fire.

"I am afraid to say that my name is no longer Azrail. My one and only name is, The Rogue," he said. "And these, are the Rogue Allegiance." He waved his hand over the hundreds of troops surrounding Ravendor. "I suggest you surrender, brother." As The Rogue said this, he spat on the ground. "I think it is in your best interest if you do." Ravendor would not be able to escape his brother and his entire army.

He looked in the direction of Amria and his six sons, and he looked right into my eyes. I knew he was looking at me because I could feel his energy flowing through me. I could hear him saying to me, "Run, get far away from here." Apparently, my mother heard it too, because after we heard his voice, she grabbed Forum's hand and told us to follow. Instead of leading us towards the Versible Portal, she guided us into an even denser part of the jungle. We could barely hear Ravendor and Azrail. I still managed to hear this exchange from my father and uncle. Cling! Clang! Clash, came the sound of their blades.

"He's just a boy, Azrail!" My father and The Rogue were locked in a deadly duel.

"His potential power is too much to pass up, Ravendor. I must have him!" The Rogue shoved Ravendor back and raised his hand to give the command to fire on his own brother. "I am afraid your insubordination is too much for me to manage. I will get your son, and I can't have you around to stop me."

Ravendor glanced behind his brother and saw the EMBT. The Reapers had rebuilt it and were using it as a high energy capacity generator. Remember how the scientists used the EMBT to be bred with the raptors those hundreds of years ago? Well, eventually a few the Reapers figured out that the cause of the explosion that completely changed the outcome of that experiment was because the EMBT couldn't handle the intense amount of energy to breed those two kinds together. Our generation knew this because those Reapers kept the data they had found in a document.

Ravendor looked at Azrail, his one and only brother, for what might have been the very last time. "Goodbye, brother," he said. The Rogue sputtered in confusion.

"Goodbye?" He was caught completely off guard. So off guard in fact, that he almost did not notice when Ravendor came up to him and hugged him.

"Yes, goodbye Azrail." Ravendor closed his eyes and threw one of his blades right at the EMBT and let go of Azrail. My father waited for the explosion. It came. It blasted everyone except The Rogue back at least one hundred yards. The blast continued farther though, and it almost reached where we were. It didn't go as far or do as much damage because we figured out a way to have the EMBT operate in a safer manner. Everyone who was knocked back by the blast was either extremely injured or already dead. My father was lying on the ground and was not moving. My mother was completely shaken, but what happened next sent shivers down all our spines. Not only did The Rogue not move from where he had been when Ravendor hugged him, but a change came over him. He completely transformed into what I would call a molten monster. His skin started cracking in different spots all over his body, and you could see red molten liquid oozing out. His skin was not a beautiful shiny black like ours, but a pale dirty black. His face no longer resembled a wolf, but more like a jack-o-lantern that was painted in the same moldy black. But, what changed the most about him was his legs and feet. In fact, you couldn't even call them feet. They were so strange looking that it is hard to describe, but for reference, think of a swirling storm of small rocks and large pebbles surrounding what looked like a translucent purple spirit. I do not know if such a thing has ever existed before, but the EMBT has been known to create weird creatures, such as me. The Rogue looked at himself in a tub of water before screaming in agony.

"Aaarrrggghhh! Ravendor did this to me? His own brother?" He shouted. "I'll get you Reapers." Then he smiled the evilest smile I have ever seen to this day. "Yes, yes, I'll return, and when I do, I'll bring an army even greater than before," he looked towards where Ravendor lay unconscious or more likely, dead. "And I'll defeat everyone in my path knowing you aren't there to stop me, Ravendor." These were his last words before he disturbingly descended into the ground, almost phasing, almost burrowing through it.

We all wanted nothing more than to run to our father and check, just to see if he was still partially alive. We hoped to spend his last moments together, but we knew that the radiation was too strong to even go near him. We were lucky it didn't go past where we were hiding. Otherwise, we might have ended up in his place as well.

Exactly four hundred years have gone by since The Rogue attacked Umbra and wiped out my people. My three oldest brothers have moved away to different planets and now are allied with The Rogue. Forum, Sunflash, and I are what stand between them and disgracing our kind. Our mother died three years ago. The planet still had too much radiation to explore the field where dozens of Reapers fell at the hand of my uncle. Sometimes I still doubt my life is real. My father and mother are both gone. My uncle is a molten rock monster that wants to conquer dimensions. My brothers are torn apart because of him. I now am going to join Magnesia Starbrand, with my army in order to fight The Rogue, who is threating her galaxy. Some people might think my life is a curse, but a wise character once said, "Every figure has a legacy. It's how we choose to live that makes it good or bad." Some people say legacies are mythical, and that the figures who live them do incredible things. I definitely have a couple of feats. I mean, I shouldn't even exist. So, I guess that makes my life story a legacy, a Reaper's Legacy.

Twangs and Flashes

BY VLAD A. MALIN

"Hey, Henry," shouted Fousel. "Do your stuff!" Henry jumped up and started running along a log, shooting arrows into targets. He jumped over a branch and continued along. He felt his bow string as he delivered shot after shot. His arrows went into the smooth wood, and with his long practice, he shot bullseye after bullseye. At last he slid down one trunk and scurried up another. He jumped, doing a few flips and landed in an athletic pose on a log. "Magnificent," whispered Fousel, "He's sure to buy it now."

Mr. Fac moved along with a couple of customers continuing to show them the reliability of his lumber. Henry took off his log costume and started retrieving his arrows. Henry worked as the mascot for Fac's Lumber, a small company in the Grellion System, in the east half of the Nexar Galaxy. He dressed up as a tree nymph and went through a routine shooting arrows and striking poses to show the strength, capabilities, and hardiness of Fac's Lumber.

"How is Henry Woodman, the fleet footed tree nymph?" said Fousel, coming up to Henry's changing room. Henry put on his brown shirt, purple pants and gray jacket, and then emerged from the room.

"Just relaxing with Fac's Lumber, tough as iron, hardy as Nexoium," responded Henry. The two friends laughed at the different slogans of Fac's Lumber. Fousel was Henry's trainer and manager regarding his

Henry Woodmen act. But to Henry, Fousel was his only real friend in a constantly changing world.

Henry's parents had been taken away when he was only an infant. The Grellian System was known for containing many rare precious metals, and there had been many crime lords mining them during the Reign of Purple-Hood. These rich barons did not have the manpower to fully exploit the potential of their land, so they had resorted to enslaving many of the peoples on nearby planets, in order to become rich. This had been the fate of Henry's parents. Thus, Henry had grown up in a strange world without any knowledge of his background. He did not even know his last name. He has been working for Fac's Lumber ever since the New Government had driven out the crime lords, and most of the Grellian System had become safe again. It was a fun job, especially because he could use his talent for archery. He had been training ever since he was a lad. Henry and Fousel went into their small cabin at the back of Mr. Fac's giant wood truck.

"Well, you could make a wooden lance or something," Fousel was saying. Henry exploded with laughter.

"You told them," said Henry, trying to catch his breath, "to make a lance!" Henry started laughing again.

"What was I supposed to tell them? They asked what effective weapons could be made with Fac's Lumber," Fousel continued. "This is the technological era. You cannot make modern weapons out of wood." Henry and Fousel laughed together and then Henry picked up a local newspaper.

"Hey," he said, "look at this. There is an archery contest about three miles from here later today."

"You want to get back to one of those?" asked Fousel.

"Well, of course, there is almost nowhere I can show off my archery skills, so I jump at the chance to do so."

"Well, you know Mr. Fac does not like your little expeditions, since they could cause delays."

"What of it? He is always so busy trying to get the customers to buy more wood. He wouldn't mind."

"You are his employee."

"Well fine, if you put it like that. I will go and ask him, and he will probably say yes."

Mr. Fac signed a few papers. Business had been slow lately. As more and more advanced technologies were introduced and made easily accessible to the public, the need for wood had slowed. Also, there was some inner feeling across the systems that war would soon emerge. Ever since the long-range communication had been cut between theirs and the other half of the galaxy, trouble seemed on the brink. All anyone wanted was better weapons and safer lodgings. And, honestly, Mr. Fac knew that there was not really much use for wood when considering those demands. Mr. Fac's thoughts were disturbed by Henry entering his office.

"Hey, Mr. Fac," he said. "Is it okay if I go down to an archery contest about three miles from here. It will not take very long. I should be back by sundown." Mr. Fac glanced up at Henry.

"Go ahead and enjoy yourself, Henry," he said. "Exercise your youth while you still have it. Don't let an old stone like me get in the way of your frivolous, carefree ways. Enjoy them while you can afford them. Oh, and take care of yourself," he said in a rush, but Henry was already out the door.

Henry moved quickly past the lumber and cabins and onto the road marked "To Hyperville." Mr. Fac had been about to start into one of his long monologues about the shortness of life and the responsibilities of the elderly, but Henry had heard it all before and decided to cut him off before he was seriously delayed. At any rate, he had been correct about what Mr. Fac would say. Fousel need not have worried about that.

Henry was now a good distance away from the base camp of Fac's Lumber. The triple suns were shining brightly, but the path was running through a thick forest, and there were immense trees that loomed over the path on either side. Because of this, the path was strewn with shadows. Fortunately, the path was level and straight, so Henry could easily see where he was going. However, the ominous nature of the shadows caused him to tremble.

He tried to not think of what might be lurking within them. He wondered why Mr. Fac was trying to sell wood here, if they were surrounded by thick forests. Couldn't these people just go and cut their own wood? Maybe they were afraid of the forest, or maybe the modern civilization simply lacked the time or the energy to go out and do such a grueling chore as cutting down trees and chopping them into usable lumber. He had heard Mr. Fac worry about people moving on from needing wood, but Henry had never thought about it before. His business was putting on a playful display for the customers, not managing the sales and profits.

The road went deeper into the forest, and now the trees were so thick overhead, that there was only a scant patch of sunlight cast at regular intervals. Just then, a cloud passed over one of the suns. For a few moments, the light was so dim that Henry could not see the ground in front of him. He waited expectantly for the light to return. Then, it was as if the ground disappeared from beneath his feet. Henry felt himself falling.

He hit the ground hard and rolled over to see that he had fallen into a pit. He vaguely saw shadowy figures moving above him. His left arm throbbed. He tried to move it, only to feel the piercing agony of pain. He heard voices above him.

"I told you that someone would come along here," one of them said.

"They would have to be a bumbling fool to not see the trap," replied another voice. "The tarp you put over the pit was a completely different shade from the ground."

"Of course, he couldn't see it," the previous one responded. "It was almost pitch black when he came along."

"How do you know it was not some animal?" said the second voice. "I would not be surprised."

"Well let's take a look then, shall we," said the first voice. "Turn on the light!"

At this point, Henry got to his feet. His arm still throbbed, but he was considering climbing out of the pit, when a bright light suddenly showed in his eyes. It took a moment for his eyes to adjust, but he was able to make out a host of figures at the top of the hole, all wearing dark cloaks and hoods. Some of them were holding swords and spears or other contraptions that resembled pistols.

"There he is, men, get him!" he heard shouted from above. He felt his body pierced in many places. Henry glanced over at his shoulder to see a needle-like object attached to a tube of blue liquid. Suddenly, Henry's consciousness wavered and blackness closed in on him.

Henry opened his eyes slowly. There was a slight pain in his arm, and the rest of his body felt weak. Henry tried to figure out where he was. He became aware that he was staring up at a metal roof. By slightly tilting his head, he could see he was in a metal chamber with a large doorway leading to the outside world. Henry could also make out hooded figures moving about outside. He noticed several other people of various shapes and sizes moving around with them.

"Hello, look who's finally conscious," came a voice from directly beside him. Henry looked up to see a medical droid holding various tools and appliances. "Hello there," said the droid. "I am V5-4Z7."

Henry rubbed his eyes, wondering what had happened. "Where am I?" he asked.

"You are in Amethyst Gorge," said the droid. "But you will hear more at the orientation, now come along." Henry sat up, bumping his head on the top of his healing capsule.

"Ouch, why is the roof so low?" he said, sliding out of his little bed. His arm was made up in a sling. The droid helped him out of the capsule and led him to the door of the chamber. He now realized that there was a large energy shield blocking the doorway, but it was transparent, so he could see what was going on outside.

The cloaked figures were moving around in the general hubbub, but all of the other people were huddled in a group at the center. They appeared to be a ragtag bunch, all wearing various articles of clothing as if they had just been out on a walk, as Henry had. Surrounding the crowd was a circle of cloaked figures, all holding laser spears. Beyond the little square was a large building, and, at the skyline, Henry could make out a tall electric fence. He shuddered trying to reason out why he was here.

A cloaked figure punched a code into a panel on the other side of the energy wall, and it went down. Immediately, two cloaked figures stepped up and guided Henry to the center of the courtyard with their laser spears. Some of the other people noticed this newest edition to their huddled group, and one came over to him.

"Hello," he said. "My name is Frank Cossel, who are you?"

"I'm Henry," said Henry.

"Just Henry?" asked Frank.

"Just Henry. Do you perhaps know where we are and why we are here?"

"Oh," said Frank. "It looks like you're already trying to figure things out, but I will tell you as much as I know. For the first question, I believe we are on some remote planet in the Grellion System. However, I am not fully sure about the answer to the second question. I do know that the cloakies (that is what I call the cloaked figures) have been capturing a lot of people and bringing them here, and I can't imagine that it is with good intentions. They brought me here about a week ago. They snagged me while I was hiking by myself. It looks like your arm is injured. Where are you from?"

"I am the mascot for Fac's Lumber, or at least I used to be. I fell into a pit and injured my arm while I was walking through the woods. They got me there." Just then, the cloakies escorted two more people into the circle and Henry heard one say,

"This is the last of the lot, bring them to the orientation." The cloakies quickly gathered around them and a tall one at the front with a red stripe on his cloak said,

"March!" He then directed them where to go while cloakies at the rear and sides prevented anyone from straying from the group. They were quickly escorted around the corner to a large iron gate, which was clearly part of a massive metal wall. The cloakies lined up behind them in a position of salute.

Suddenly, an ominous figure with a black cape appeared on the top of the iron gate. He stepped forward and spoke.

"Greetings, hikers, hunters, and other figures of the Grellion System in which I have taken an interest. I am Ruthard Scott, and I am the reason you are here. Welcome to the planet, Kalua, specifically to the great facility of Amethyst Gorge. This location is remote and most unsupportive of life, so I can assure you that there is no chance that anyone will ever find you here. I will also gladly inform you that you will never leave. You may be wondering why I have taken you here and what you will be doing, which I will tell you. This, friends, is what is commonly called an interstellar space mine. Some of you may have heard of the great mines of the Grellion System and might be wondering, especially from the name of this place, 'What shining, brilliant crystals will we be uncovering from the rocky soil?'" Ruthard reached into his pocket and pulled out a small bag and poured out a white, sand-like substance.

"This is what you will be digging," he said. "Sodium Chloride, or, you may know it as, salt. Yes, friends, I hope you are not disappointed in finding that you are to work in a salt mine. If you are, well, I would suggest keeping that to yourself. For, I can assure you that you will grow to love the work. In case you were wondering, this mine is surrounded by steep, thousand-foot-high rock walls. Beyond that is a high-powered electric fence that generates a force field over the entire mine. Beyond that is the barren, desolate surface of Kalua. There is no chance of ever escaping, and any attempt to do so or to go beyond the boundaries set by the supervisors (those are my cheerful friends who will help you get used to your new life), will raise my extreme displeasure. Any such workers shall no longer work nor will they continue to exist. However, I have high hopes that none of you will raise my displeasure. I would certainly recommend embracing your new life with your whole heart and mind. And now, with no further words of wisdom, your new life shall begin." The large iron gates slowly creaked open.

The prisoners were led through the iron gates, and they now saw a wide stretch of terrain leading away to the far wall. This whole area was covered with many holes and valleys, where Henry saw lots of other people mining salt. The salt was pressed into large blocks, which were stacked on either side of the gate.

The group was taken out to a large flat area, where the cloakie with the red stripe divided them into three different groups: mining the salt, shaping it into blocks, and carrying the blocks to the wall. Henry was assigned to shaping the salt into blocks, and he was glad to see that Frank was also assigned to this field.

They were once again escorted along by the cloakies, this time over a long distance to the far end of the mining area. Henry and Frank, along with several other people, were sent over to a large pile of salt, which they began to shape into blocks. This was done with a distinct process that involved wrapping the salt with cloth, and then binding it with rope. This was rather difficult for Henry, with his arm in a sling. However, he was able to move along decently, with Frank's help.

They continued at this work for several hours, and Henry became extremely hot, tired, and thirsty. The large pile of salt at the far end of their working area never seemed to reduce in size, because the miners produced more salt at the same rate the packagers could bundle it.

After some time, the cloakie allowed everyone to take a brief break, and they were provided with a few bites to eat, and a sip of water. The food did not taste very good, nor did the water, which was partially due to poor quality, and partially due to the salty air, but it was something. After about a fifteen-minute break, the cloakies ordered them back to work, and they began again. Henry could see that Frank was becoming extremely bored of the slow tedious process. Trying to be positive, he asked, "So, what were you doing before you came here?"

"Well," said Frank. "I wanted to be a spaceship engineer when I was young, and I studied as much as I could for that, but my family was rather poor, and I had a hard time getting a job with so little experience. But I like the outdoor world, and I hiked a lot. I come from the planet Hitita, which is known for its strange geological formations and peaceful nature scenes. I started my own business as a tour guide, and I showed people all sorts of natural wonders on the planet, but I was often going out by myself to find new undiscovered corners. It was on one such occasion that I stepped on a net and was taken here. This place is desolate and so barren. I have often longed to see just one natural scene the past week. What about you?"

Henry thought for a moment. "I grew up on the planet, Marentus, which has lots of water and trees, but I grew bored of it eventually, and I wanted to see the world. My parents disappeared when I was very young. In fact, most people think they were taken to a place very much like this. One time, a man came to my planet, trying to sell wood. He was impressed by my skills in archery and offered to give me a job as his mascot."

"So you are an archer," said Frank.

"Yes," said Henry. "I was considering joining the army, but Mr. Fac (that was the man who was selling wood) gave me an opportunity to see the world with much less danger to myself. I took up his offer. Traveling with him and practicing archery made me happy for some time, but I recently have begun to want something more, and look where that got me." A cloakie approached Frank and Henry.

"I want to see less talk and more salt blocks," he shouted at them and grabbed Frank by the shoulder. He pulled him over to a different area, away from Henry. Another prisoner was moved over to work with Henry.

"Well, what's your name?" asked Henry, as soon as the cloakie had moved away. The new person grunted and turned away from Henry, evidently trying to avoid what had just happened to Frank. Henry kept to himself for the rest of the day, but he found it very wearisome without his new friend.

As the sun was finally going down, the cloakies rounded up the prisoners and marched them off to a large area at the edge of the mining zone, which had numerous buildings on it. The workers were then divided up into each building. The new workers, which included Henry and Frank, were guided to a few buildings which had evidently been constructed more recently than the others. Within the lodging house, there was a central hallway which had individual cells on either side. These cells all had wide doorways and transparent energy fields to serve as doors, like the medical chamber where Henry had woken up. The workers were assigned to a cell in pairs of two. Henry was overjoyed when he and Frank were put into the same cell.

Within the cell, they found another meager crust of bread, along with a few sips of water for their dinner. The cells were completely bare, except for the two mats, which were fastened to the floor on either side, as well as two pairs of clothes laid out for them. These looked very much like prison clothes. They were tan with a large number on the back of the shirt. Henry's number was 4102, while Frank's was 4101. Henry and Frank ate their dinner silently, but after they had finished, Frank said sarcastically, "Well, these are nice living conditions."

"I guess we will have to get used to them," said Henry. "That Ruthard Scott guy did say we would be here for the rest of our lives."

"Well, we can hope that his statement proves not entirely correct," said Frank.

"I don't think so," said Henry. "I have heard of places like these before. If you remember, my parents were believed to be taken to one. There are always stories of people disappearing, never to be found again. We might actually spend the rest of our lives here."

"Well, I prefer not to think about it. Let's talk about something else."

"What would you be doing on a particular night like this?"

"Sometimes, on an especially cold night, my whole family would gather together in our living room. We would have a large fire in the fireplace and tell stories about mysterious goings on out in the cold darkness."

"What goings on would you talk about?"

"Well, my favorite were the tales of The Bolte."

"The Bolte?"

"Yes, The Bolte. He is a mysterious figure that appears to lost and weary travelers with a flash of red light. He helps them find food and shelter."

"That's interesting. What else would they say about The Bolte?"

Frank continued to tell Henry of the mysterious Bolte, until the lights went out, and they had to go to bed. Both of them were greatly comforted by thoughts of their own homes, however far away they were now, and they slept soundly.

They woke the next morning to bright lights and a loud noise coming from the walls, like an alarm clock. The energy fields were soon turned off and the workers were marched out. They were also ordered to turn in whatever clothes they had been wearing when they arrived, and now wear only the provided clothes with large numbers. They had a meager breakfast and then proceeded out to the mines.

This day passed much as the one before, as well as the one following, and the one after that. Henry got used to the pattern of working and eating, but he always looked forward to his talks with Frank at the end of the day. They discussed many things together in those dark hours, like tales of the Bolte, and other stories. Sometimes they related their own thoughts and feelings or interesting things that had occurred during the day, though this was rare. After many days of the same dull pattern, they soon lost track of how long they had been in Amethyst Gorge.

Henry's arm was soon back in working order, and he was able to go about without wearing the sling, and use his arm just as well as ever. One day, as he joined the team who packaged salt, he was approached by a cloakie with a red stripe.

"Worker 4102," said the cloakie. Henry looked at him in surprise. He had never been addressed by a cloakie before. "Seeing as you are medically recovered," the cloakie continued. "You are being transferred to the mining area. Now, join the mining team."

Henry moved over to the mining team. There, he was given a shovel, a pick, and a bag for carrying salt. The miners were sent into the rocky valleys and holes. The other miners all had their usual spots, which they found very quickly. Henry had to go some way before he found an open area. He was now very near the steep cliff which served as the border of Amethyst Gorge.

Henry could see that there were many cloakies patrolling the mining area, to ensure that no miners tried to leave their stations. However, there were very few near the far edge of this sector. He found a dark cleft from which no one could see him. This area did not have very much salt, so few people ever went there. Henry was glad to be able to catch his breath and find some shield from the bright sun, but after sitting there for a few minutes, he determined that he should probably get to work.

There was a little salt in his small cleft, and he started shoveling it into his bag. He soon hit a large rock, but there seemed to be salt behind it, so he worked at it with his pick. The rock was very tough, but after working at it for some time, Henry was able to make a crack. He was astonished when he saw a faint red glow shining through the crack. Henry quickly hacked the rock away, to reveal a small red crystal that shone with its own light.

Just then, Henry heard footsteps coming towards him. He quickly grabbed the red crystal and shoved it into his pocket. Another miner came into view.

"Hullo there," he said. "You found a real quiet cleft there, eh." Henry nodded. "There's not much salt here, fella, so I would recommend trying a spot a little closer to the salt bundling area." With that, the other miner stumped off in the direction he had come from.

Henry made sure the crystal was secure, and then he left his little cleft, but he made note of it, so that he could find it again if needed.

Henry mined a lot of salt that day, and he soon understood how the miners had been able to continuously keep the pile of salt in the packaging area at a substantial size. Henry did not go near his secret cleft throughout that day, but he was very excited to show Frank his discovery in the evening. Frank was also extremely interested in the shining red crystal. "Wow! That's amazing," he said, when Henry first showed it to him. "Where did you find it?"

"I was digging in a dark cleft at the far end of the mining fields, when I uncovered it," said Henry. "There was not very much salt there, so I think I understand why no one else had found it."

"Do you think there are any more gems there?" asked Frank.

"I don't know," replied Henry. "I left the little cleft right after I found these crystals, but I could probably find it again." Frank poured over the crystal for some time.

"I have read a little about rocks and minerals," he said at last. "And I do believe this is a Keblar crystal."

"What does that mean?" asked Henry

"Keblar crystals are very rare and valuable. They were sometimes used as currency by the ancients."

"Very interes..." said Henry, but before he could finish, he was suddenly cut off by a loud alarm, and the lights blacked out. Henry and Frank quickly got on their mats and hid the crystal. They heard lots of shouts and footsteps from outside the lodging house. A few cloakies walked down the central hallway checking every cell. After a full sweep, they seemed satisfied, and left. The noise outside soon died down, but Henry heard the loud creak of the large iron gates opening and closing.

Henry and Frank woke up the following morning to the sound of the alarm, but the lights did not come on. The workers were escorted out of the lodging houses as usual, but Henry thought the cloakies were viewing the workers with far more suspicion than normal, and they kept a tight hold on their laser spears.

Instead of being led to their various sectors and work zones as usual after breakfast, the entire body assembled in front of the large iron gate. The cloakies stood in a position of salute as Ruthard Scott once again appeared on top of the large iron gate. He seemed less pleased and more upset than when Henry had seen him previously.

"Hello, faithful workers," he said, adopting his usual tone. "Some of you may have been awakened by a disturbance that occurred early last night. Some of you may have even known what was going on, but I will explain anyway. A certain few disruptive residents adopted the foolish plan of trying to escape Amethyst Gorge. However, we know all that goes on in this place. The fools who attempted to escape were caught and dealt with. Now, they will serve as an example to the rest of you."

Just then, some latches opened near the top of the iron gate, and several poles emerged with limp bodies dangling from them. "Anyone who tries to do something similar to these insolent fools will meet the same fate." Ruthard Scott went back into the tall building behind the wall, and the cloakies guided all of the workers to their usual areas.

Henry thought about this attempted escape often throughout the following days. He thought he understood how those workers could be driven to make a desperate escape plan, but he did not know how they thought they could get through the army of cloakies and the iron wall. He discussed this with Frank during some of their evenings, and Frank could not make sense of it either. There was not much of interest taking place for the workers in Amethyst Gorge, so events like the attempted escape were long remembered.

It was some time later that an announcement was made to the workers. New lodging houses were to be built. Anyone with some knowledge of electronics or welding was directed to join a fourth group of workers at the beginning of the day, in order to aid in the construction. Frank, having taken some education to be a spaceship designer, joined this fourth group. He was a patient person, but he had grown increasingly bored of doing the same thing all day every day, and he was glad to try something new.

Henry had never really found an interest in things of that sort, preferring archery and woodworking. Also, mining was less tedious than packaging, though it did often get wearisome for Henry. He had not returned to his secret cleft where he found the Keblar crystal, but he always kept the jewel on him, for he knew the cloakies searched all the rooms while the workers were away.

However, Henry was very interested in the construction of the new lodging house, and he would often ask Frank about it in the night. "How do all of the force field doors work?" he asked on one of these particular nights.

"Well," said Frank. "The energy fields are projected by transmitters in the door frame, which are electronically controlled from a central circuit box at the edge of the lodging complex. Most energy doors are controlled by a panel beside the doorway, but this system is unique in that all the controls are in a single location."

"Interesting," said Henry. "Maybe that was how those guys who tried to escape thought they could make it. If you cut all of the energy doors at the same time, then all of the workers could quickly amass into a unified force. If they could catch the cloakies off guard, theycould have a reasonable chance of escaping."

Frank thought for a moment. "I wonder what went wrong," he finally said.

"Maybe the cloakies saw it coming," responded Henry.

"I guess that could have happened," said Frank. "But it still doesn't make sense." Henry and Frank continued to ponder this until they went to sleep, and it remained in their minds more prominently than everything else during the work day.

The days proceeded like this for some time until one evening when Frank told Henry that the new lodging houses were complete, and he would resume packaging salt the following day. "It will be hard getting back to that drearysome packaging business tomorrow," Frank said rather glumly on this particular night.

"Ah, cheer up Frank," said Henry. "I have been hard at it in the mines this whole time."

"But it is not the same for you," said Frank. "Mining has far more variation and excitement to it. Packaging is just doing the same thing over and over again all day."

"I know how it is," said Henry, thinking back to those early days when he had a sprained arm. "But, you should be glad you had a change in routine." Frank got over his own sourness, and he prepared for salt packaging the next day.

It was on this following day that another batch of workers arrived. Henry and Frank probably should have realized that the only reason they were building new lodging houses was because new workers would need them. However, this had not occurred to them until they saw a large collection of new faces wearing typical hiking clothes like they had worn on their first day. Henry did not really care much about the new load of workers. He just settled into his work as he usually did. However, the new miners were assigned to an area near Henry's group. It so happened that, as Henry walked toward the spot where he had been working, he passed one of the new workers, who stopped in his tracks and stared at Henry with his mouth wide open.

"Henry!?" he stammered.

Henry looked at this person and gasped. "Fousel!"

Fousel and Henry gazed at each other in shock.

At last, Henry stammered, "Why...? How...?"

"Get back to work!" shouted a cloakie walking nearby. Henry and Fousel quickly hastened back to their work, but they kept an eye on each other for the rest of the day. At last, Henry found himself a bit separated from the other miners, and there were no cloakies nearby. He was once again approached by his old friend. They ducked under a cleft of rock and looked each other up and down.

"How did you get here?" Henry finally said.

"First, I think you should say how you got here," replied Fousel. "I have been searching for you for the past four months, ever since you went missing."

"Four months!" said Henry in surprise. "It felt like eternity."

"It has been a very worrisome time," said Fousel. "What with you being missing and all. What happened the day of the archery contest, when I saw you last?"

"I was just walking along towards town, when I fell into a pit and was captured and taken here. How is Mr. Fac, and how did you get here?"

"Uncle Fac and I were determined to find you after the people at the archery contest said you never arrived. We searched the path and found a pit in the middle of the road. I discovered a tranquilizer dart at the bottom. There were a lot of footprints around the hole, leading away into the woods. We tried our best to follow the trail, but the woods were thick, and it was very rough terrain. We almost got lost multiple times out in those dark woods. Uncle Fac eventually became sick. He was ill for a week, and he couldn't go out with me. His condition appeared to be getting worse and worse. Something deep down inside told me that he would only recover if he saw you alive and well. One day, I went very deep into the woods, further than I ever remember going, and then I saw a spaceship fly over my head and land nearby. I followed the noise until I came to a clearing. There were a lot of hooded figures moving around it, and when they saw me, they shot me with a tranquilizer dart.

I recognized it as the same one I found in the pit. Then they took me to this place."

"That's terrible!" said Henry. "You really think Mr. Fac is not going to get better."

"Oh!" exclaimed Fousel, as if in pain. "I have been trying not to think about it. With me gone too, he is likely to die!" Henry gazed at Fousel in horror. Henry had thought sometimes about his old friends during the past few months, but his thoughts mainly consisted of them continuing in the happy life he had once shared with them. The thought of them living with worry and sickness had never occurred to him.

"What are we going to do?" he finally stammered.

"We have to get out of here," said Fousel

"But how?" asked Henry.

"I don't know, but there must be some way," said Fousel. "You have been here far longer than me. Do you have any ideas?"

Henry recalled the group that had tried to escape Amethyst Gorge recently. He and Frank had often theorized about how these workers had tried to pull it off. A number of thoughts came into his mind about how an escape plan could be made and successfully carried out. "I think I might have an idea," he said at last. "But we should get back to work for the moment. We don't want the cloakies (that's what I call them) to suspect anything."

Henry and Fousel quickly got back to work, and did not go near each other again for the rest of the day, but Henry continued to formulate his plan of escape, which he had suddenly found the determination to make. He approached Frank that evening.

"Well, what's new today?" asked Frank.

"One of the new workers was my old friend Fousel," responded Henry.

"Really," said Frank. "That's interesting."

Henry took a deep breath. "I have something very important to tell you, Frank," he said.

"What is it?" asked Frank, surprised at Henry's somber tone.

"I have made the decision to escape from Amethyst Gorge."

Frank looked at Henry in shock. "What!? Why?" was all he could manage to say.

"Fousel told me that Mr. Fac has been sick and is close to death. He thinks Mr. Fac will die of grief after losing both of us. Out of respect for him and what he did for me, and out of respect for his nephew, my close friend, Fousel, I consider it my duty. It would please me greatly if you also aided in our escape, but you do not have to join me. In honor of our friendship, I ask that you not reveal this to anyone."

Frank looked at Henry for a long time in silence. At last, he held up his hand and shook Henry's, saying, "I'm sick of this place anyway. So how are we going to escape?"

"I have thought about that," said Henry. "And I think the best way is to utilize the plan we theorized before. We willvturn off all of the cell doors at once. Then we will overrun the cloakies and escape."

"I guess that is the best plan, but how are we going to get to the central control box at night, and how are we going to get over the iron wall?"

"I don't know exactly how yet," replied Henry. "But that is why I wanted your help. You now know a lot about how these lodging houses work, and you are skilled at making elaborate plans."

Frank laughed, and said, "I guess you're right." He sat on his bed and started thinking hard. "I guess the first issue is turning off the energy doors, which we could pull off if someone hid outside the cell until darkness."

"The cloakies have really tightened their protocol since the last escape attempt," said Henry, shaking his head. "It would be almost impossible to stay out of the cell without their noticing."

"We could try to get out after everyone has been put in the cells."

"But the only way to turn off the energy doors is from the central control box."

Frank looked about the cell. "The walls are all metal, so it's no use trying to make a hole," he said. "Maybe if we could make some sort of explosion..." Frank brightened up.

"What is it?" asked Henry.

"I think I know exactly what we can do," replied Frank.

Henry and Frank woke up the next morning and proceeded as usual to breakfast. The whole group did not spend very much time together, but Henry snaked his way through the crowd pulling himself and Frank right up to Fousel.

"Hello, Fousel," said Henry. "This is my friend Frank. He is joining our operation."

"Glad to meet you," said Fousel, shaking hands with Frank. "Unfortunately, I was just informed that I will be moved to the salt transportation group, so we will not be able to have extensive conversations."

"That's okay," said Henry. "We can communicate, when possible, like right now. We are currently developing a plan."

"Interesting," said Fousel. "Fill me in later." Fousel went off to join the salt hauling group, and Henry and Frank also went to their respective areas.

As the work got started, Henry strayed away from the rest of the miners. He went into the more remote area at the far end of the mining zone. He looked around to make sure no cloakies were watching him and made his way toward the secret cleft. He was now glad he had memorized the location of this hole, because, even though the ground in this more remote area had changed little due to its lack of salt, the terrain all looked the same, and it was hard to find the same place twice. Henry at last made his way to the deep, cool cleft where he had found the crystal. As he expected, there was no evidence that anyone had been there since his last visit.

Once all this was assured, Henry began to deepen and expand the hole. It was not long before he found more Keblar crystals, and after working for half an hour he had quite a pile of them. This was something he and Frank had discussed the previous night. Keblar crystals, Frank had explained, while definitely valued for their scarcity and red glow, also emitted energy, which could be channeled into a strong burst. Frank had said they are often used in energy weapons. This was how they planned to disable their shield door, after it had been shut.

Once Henry thought he had enough of these crystals, he hid them in various places around his body. The prison suit only had two pockets, one of which he was already using for the first Keblar crystal, but Henry was able to manage by placing crystals in his sleeves, shoes, and other places. At last, he moved out, and resumed his salt mining.

Henry continued to work, until he joined the other miners for their lunch break. From his place, he could see Frank, eating with the other salt packagers. Henry carefully watched as Frank took up his cup of water, but seemingly, accidentally spilled most of it on the ground. This was Henry's signal, and as soon as they finished their lunch break, he quickly made his way to a shallow hole near the salt bundling area, where he was presently joined by Frank.

"All went well," said Henry, revealing a red glow coming out of his pocket.

"Well," said Frank. "I guess it's time for the risky part." Frank and Henry looked out of the shallow hole to observe the nearby cloakies. There was a group of them heading off into the mining area, while another bunch of them sat, observing the workers packaging salt.

When they thought the cloakies were not looking in their direction, Frank and Henry made off quickly and silently. They stole around the outer edge of the mining area until they arrived at the lodging houses. They had to be extremely cautious, as there were more cloakies about in the lodging area, but they were able to avoid most of the danger.

Frank directed them to the pile of leftover scrap that had not been cleared out yet. Most of this scrap had been thrown into a large crate at the side of the lodging area. After once again making sure there were no cloakies around, Frank and Henry approached the side of the bin. It was ten feet high, but Henry was able to help Frank up. Once inside the bin, he began sorting through the refuse, looking for useful parts. Henry stood at the base of the large bin and listened for footsteps. He was almost sure the coast was clear, when he heard low voices approaching. He had just enough time to dart behind a nearby rock, while two cloakies came into view.

"The work of patrolling the slaves is still going smoothly." one of them was saying. "There has not been any fuss since the last escape attempt, and we have been watching them far more closely."

"Good, good," said the other. "We just don't want that to happen again. Pay dropped a good percentage after those nuisances almost caused real trouble."

"No, I can quite assure that will not happen again," replied the other. "But I haven't seen this side of the barrier lately, what's been going on?"

"Nothing of significance," the cloakie said, appearing to try to seem important. "We are just preparing for the boss's party in three days."

"Really," said the first. "The annual celebration where the boss invites his friends over for a spectacular feast? I hadn't realized that time was coming round again."

"Well, it is, and the boss likes to have a host of guards there to impress the guests," the other cloakie continued. "I bet he'll put you way out with the slaves, as far from the guests as possible," he said with a laugh.

"You know just as well as I that the boss is inviting his primary investors. He wants to show an air of security, and almost all of the guards will be present. There's only going to be a few out here, and I'll be cursed, if I'm one of them."

The two continued like this as they slowly sauntered back towards the iron wall, but Henry saw a window of opportunity. He went back over to the crate and helped Frank out.

"Did you get the stuff?" asked Henry.

"Yes," said Frank, showing Henry some various metal parts. "What were those cloakies doing?"

"They were just talking. Did you hear what they said?"

"No, what was it?"

"They said that there is going to be a large event going on in three days, and most of the cloakies will be in attendance."

"I guess we know when we are going to try to pull this thing off." The two quickly made their way back to their stations, and pretended as if they had never gone away. This was rather easy for Henry and no one suspected anything. They continued their physical labor for the rest of the day, but their minds were at work far more than usual. At the end of the day, they had another encounter with Fousel.

"We did some scouting and retrieving today," whispered Henry. "A large amount of cloakies will be assembled at a party three days from now. That will be go time."

"That's great," said Fousel. "I had my first day with this salt block carrying, and it is hard work."

"Do you stack the salt blocks against the wall?" asked Frank.

"Yes, we do," responded Fousel.

"Could you stack the salt blocks in a down sloping pattern away from the wall?"

"I guess I could try."

"Good."

They separated again to go to their lodging houses. As soon as the cloakies had all gone away, Frank took out the scrap metal, and Henry revealed all of the Keblar crystals. Under the faint red light, Frank attempted to build a strange small device. He worked long into the night, but he could not finish, and so they hid all evidence of their work, and went to sleep.

The next two days went by without many events of consequence, but for Henry, every hour was filled with all sorts of thoughts about their chances of escaping, and what he would do if they succeeded, and what he would do if they did not. He knew that Fousel and he would return to that wooded planet where they had left Mr. Fac, but deep-down Henry feared the Mr. Fac was already dead, and if he was, what then? Henry could not really answer these questions at present, but he determined to focus on the current situation. If they were able to rally the prisoners into one force and take hold of Amethyst Gorge, what then? They were not exactly a united force, and there would probably be a vast number of different opinions. Ruthard Scott might have other allies which would come in great numbers to defeat their measly band of ragtag prisoners, and enslave them once again. Henry could not really answer his own questions, but overthrowing Ruthard and his men took the highest priority in his mind. He would figure the rest out later.

Fousel was in much more frustration and agitation than Frank and Henry, as the salt block hauling required all the physical labor of mining, while having all the tediousness of salt packaging. Fousel also did not like submitting to the cloakies. He met up with Frank and Henry on the second day, clearly upset.

"What's the matter, Fousel?" asked Henry.

"That silly cloakie saw the way I was stacking salt blocks and ordered me to restack them," said Fousel, angrily. "He literally wanted me to grab the blocks which had already been set, and place them only a few yards away. I tried to explain that they were good where they were, but he wouldn't listen."

"Be careful," said Frank. "We do not want them to suspect we are up to something."

"I try," replied Fousel. "But sometimes their orders make no sense."

The three went to bed, knowing that all their hopes and fears would be met the following day. They knew this might be the last sleep of their lives. Frank and Henry arrived at breakfast the next morning, trying their best to appear normal. They might have been noticed, but many of the cloakies were keeping down their own excitement over the coming celebration that night.

However, Frank and Henry's spirits were checked when, try as they might, they could not find Fousel. They had searched the whole crowd twice over, when a rather short and thin worker approached them.

"If you're looking for your friend," he said. "They took him away." Henry and Frank stared at him in shock. "He had a too rebellious nature," he continued, shaking his head. Seeing that he would get no response from Frank and Henry, and not really wanting to anyway, this worker quickly disappeared into the crowd again.

Frank and Henry could hardly accept what had happened as they went off to their respective working areas. Henry continued to think about Fousel for the rest of the day. Though he was very sad at Fousel's disappearance, he determined that, in respect of his friend, he now must act upon his plan. It was with sadness and excitement that he met Frank at the end of the day.

"What do you think happened to Fousel?" asked Frank

"Nothing good," said Henry. "They could have killed him, or they could have tortured him, if they suspected he was part of a conspiracy."

"Do you think we should continue with the plan?" asked Frank.

Henry looked at Frank for some time. He could see the worry in Frank's face. This was what he had been afraid of as well, but he had already made his decision. "In honor of Fousel," said Henry at last. "And in honor of Mr. Fac, and my parents, and all of the workers here, I consider it my duty to act upon the plan. We may never get another chance like this, and even if Fousel was forced to reveal our plan, we are certain to die either way. I personally have hope that they will have postponed such actions as torture and murder until after their celebration, but I will once again inform you, this danger is what I am bringing upon myself. You do not have to join me, though I hope you will. You can make your own decision."

Frank stood up next to Henry with a new confidence. "You are right Henry," he said. "This is our best chance and there is still time. Now is the time to act!"

Frank pulled some various pieces of machinery and electronics out of his pockets and sleeves and quickly began to assemble them into a device with some buttons on one side and a tube sticking out the other. When this device was fully constructed, it was about the size of a large dictionary, and about the weight of one as well.

"This is it," said Frank. "But one more thing." Frank pulled out a smaller tube that resembled a flashlight. "There was a little bit of scrap left over and I decided to make a miniature version." He handed the tube to Henry. "You will make better use of it than me."

"Thank you," said Henry. "Now, let's get out of here."

Frank held up his device to a mark on the cell wall beside the door. He switched it on, and a large red laser came out of the tube, blasting through the wall. Frank quickly turned it off, as the energy door sputtered on and off a few times, and then disappeared.

"I hit the cable giving power to the energy door," said Frank. "Go time."

Henry and Frank walked out of the cell and went down the hallway to the doorway leading out of the lodging house. They looked around to make sure no cloakies were nearby, and then quietly proceeded out. They made their way to their central control box. There were a group of cloakies standing by the door, talking to themselves.

Henry took his laser device, and approached them from one side. One of the cloakies saw him and activated his laser spear, but it was too late. The cloakies had been standing in a row by the door, and when Henry turned on his laser, it blasted all of them. Henry and Frank stepped over the bodies. The door was locked, and there was a keypad by the knob.

"Let's blast it," said Henry.

"No, no, no," said Frank. "We might damage the stuff inside."

"Well, what are we going to do?" said Henry.

"I have an idea," said Frank, and he went behind the control building. Henry looked down at the dead cloakies, and saw that one of them had been reading a book. He picked it up, and saw the title, *The Appellis 650 Coordination and Communication Wristband: Description and Verbal Demonstration*. There was also a picture of a wristband with buttons on it, which Henry identified as the wristband which all the cloakies wore and used to communicate with each other.

"This could be useful," said Henry, and he flipped to a page with an image of the wristband, and arrows pointing to all of the different buttons and explaining their function.

Just then Frank returned from behind the control building. "I think I can disable the energy doors from behind the control box," he said.

"That's great," said Henry. "But look what I discovered." Henry pointed to the image in the book. "We can use the wristbands to lure all the cloakies on this side of the wall to a single place."

"That is quite a discovery," said Frank.

"Here," said Henry. "Help me drag these bodies behind the control box." Frank and Henry pulled the bodies of the dead cloakies behind the building, and then Henry took one of the wristbands and pressed the button, which the book had labeled "summoning". It would gather everyone wearing a wristband within a quarter mile radius. Soon enough, a large group of about fifteen cloakies emerged into the clearing in front of the control building, and looked in surprise at the unguarded door. These cloakies met the same fate as the first ones.

Meanwhile, Frank had returned to the back of the control building, where he had previously spotted an exposed wire. He knew this connected the control panel to the other lodging houses, and he was pretty sure it powered the cell doors. Looking now, he realized that there were actually two wires, one red and the other green. After observing more closely, he noticed that the green wire had been cut and later repaired. Frank thought back to the night when the other workers had tried to escape. He remembered how the lights had suddenly gone out. Frank realized the lights were also universally controlled from a single point.

"I know why they didn't succeed," said Frank to himself. "They cut the wrong wire." Frank took out a small piece of sharpened metal and cut through the red wire, which controls the energy doors. "That should do it," he thought.

Frank joined Henry in front of the control building, where there was quite a heap of dead cloakies. "I think I finished them off," said Henry. "This area is secure."

"That's great," said Frank. "Let's gather the other prisoners." Henry and Frank went into the now unguarded lodging houses, and told those inside to come out, as their freedom was at hand. There was soon quite a large crowd of people in the center of the lodging area, many confused, and none knowing what had happened. At last, the group quieted down as they saw Frank and Henry coming to the center.

"Hello fellow prisoners, I am Henry, and this is Frank. We have, this very night, escaped from our cell, defeated some of the cloakies, and released all of you as well. We were able to do this through careful preparation, and because there were very few cloakies guarding us at this time. Ruthard Scott is having a celebration on the other side of the wall, and most of the cloakies are there. We now have the opportunity to take over Amethyst Gorge. There are still a good many cloakies on the other side of the wall, but we outnumber them greatly. If you are worried or afraid, I will now remind you that you were all forcibly taken here, and made to work against your will. You all know there is no hope of us being released. Is it not a better end to fall while trying to escape, than to live out the rest of your days in slavery? If you are with the escape attempt, proceed to the iron gate with Frank and myself. Proceed in stealth, for we do not quite yet want our enemies to know what is afoot. From there we will fall upon Ruthard and his men in their celebration and capture them before they know what has happened. Let us go!"

With this, Henry began to make his way to the edge of the crowd. They would have let out a great cheer, but for his warning to be silent, and Henry received many a smile and an encouraging word as he passed to the front. Then, Frank and he led the group along to the main gate.

Once there, Henry, and several of the nimblest prisoners climbed up the pile of salt blocks, which was still mostly as Fousel had left it. When they reached the top, theywere able to help each other onto the top of the wall.

Henry and four others were soon there, and began to make their way to the gate, when suddenly, they were attacked by a group of cloakies. Henry found himself on his back with a laser spear at his neck.

"You will not succeed in this revolt!" said the cloakie, whom Henry noticed had a red stripe on his cloak. "You are weak slaves and cannot escape our superior forces!"

For a moment, Henry thought he was lost, but then he remembered the small laser device Frank had given him. It was just inside his sleeve, and he quickly slid it into his hand. "Take a bite of this," said Henry. This laser was far smaller than Frank's other design, so it did not have the same fatal effect, but it still ripped a hole through the red striped cloakie. The cloakie screamed in pain, and then stumbled backwards, tripping on the edge off the walkway and falling off the high wall.

The other cloakies hesitated for a moment when they saw their leader's demise, and the other prisoners, recovering from their own surprise, now fought back with a savage fervor that caught the cloakies off guard. Despite being better armed, they were soon overpowered.

Henry and the rest then made their way to the gate. Henry found a lever held in place by a heavy lock, but he was able to remove it with his laser. He then pulled the lever, and the heavy iron gates slowly creaked open.

Henry went down a set of stairs on the inside of the gate, where he joined Frank at the head of a large body of escaped prisoners. "What's next," said Henry?

"I guess this is as far as we planned," said Frank. "But that was the hard part. Hey, look!," he said, pointing to a nearby building. "That building says 'Armory'. We should have the other workers arm themselves.

Henry went out in front of the people swarming through the gate. "Come on, everyone," he said, "into the armory. Let everyone who has strength arm himself." He led the people into the armory, where they found a large supply of laser spears, laser guns, and energy crossbows. Everyone began to grab weapons, and Henry selected an energy crossbow. He rejoined Frank, who was standing guard.

"The coast is clear," said Frank. "There were not any cloakies here. I think they all might have been part of the force that surprised you on the wall."

"That's great," said Henry. "Let's make for the main hall." The escaped workers now assembled outside the armory and moved towards the Central Hall, where Ruthard was entertaining his guests. There were a few guards by the doors, but they knew what was happening, they were filled with laser bolts. Henry directed a host of escaped prisoners to the roof, while the rest approached the front door. With a nod to his companions, Henry pushed the doors to the Central Hall wide open. He was met with a scene of luxury and elegance. At the center of the room sat Ruthard Scott and his other guests, all wearing elaborate clothing and enjoying a most exquisite meal. A professional band played mellow jazz at the back of the room. There were three groups of cloakies at the perimeter of the room. Most were sitting with their weapons trying to give off an air of security, while others were still eating. To the immense astonishment of the prisoners, they had their hoods off. As soon as Henry stepped in, everyone looked at him, and the music stopped.

At a gesture from Ruthard, the group of cloakies nearest to the door grabbed their laser spears and moved toward Henry and the prisoners. Before they could take ten steps, as they were torn to pieces by a rain of fire from the upper windows.

"Hello, Ruthard Scott," said Henry. "We are here to oversee a change in management of Amethyst Gorge. There will be no more slavery or abduction, and everyone will be free to come and go as they please. That being said, you and your men must face justice. Anyone who resists will be killed. Under the new authority, you are ordered to lay down your weapons and be escorted to confinement."

Ruthard glared at Henry for some time, but he could see the figures in the upper windows had their weapons aimed at him. At last, he said, "So be it."

At this, the cloakies began to line up and lay their weapons in the center of the room. Ruthard and his guests huddled together. Henry now saw a young man sitting by Ruthard and talking with him. Henry thought they might be family, due to their similar appearance.

Ruthard suddenly gave a sharp whistle. All of the cloakies attacked the prisoners with ferocious strength. They caught the prisoners off guard, and it was difficult for the sentinels on the roof to distinguish friend from foe. A group of four cloakies moved toward Frank and Henry, but they were hit with Frank's laser. Henry and Frank quickly began to assist their fellow prisoners, when Henry noticed Ruthard disappearing into a trap door.

"Frank!" said Henry. "Ruthard is getting away!"

Frank and Henry quickly moved toward the trap door, shooting cloakies who tried to bar their way. It was well camouflaged, but since Henry knew where to look, they quickly found it. Frank opened the hatch to reveal a deep passage and a ladder. Henry swiftly climbed down, with Frank just above him.

They were now in a very dark stone passageway that sloped downhill. Fortunately, Henry had taken a helmet with a light from the armory. He switched on the light, so it was not pitch dark, and they were able to make their way forward.

After going along some way, a dim light became visible from around a curve in the path. They were just about to round to the corner, when they were confronted with laser spear. A voice said, "Drop the weapons!"

Henry put down his energy crossbow, and Frank set down the laser device. A group of cloakies emerged, along with Ruthard and the young man.

"Not so strong without all your friends behind you," said Ruthard. "Now you will experience the true punishment of an attempted escape. Bring them along." The cloakies grabbed Henry's energy crossbow and Frank laser device, and then dragged them around the corner.

Henry now saw that the light had been coming from a river of lava flowing along underground. They were currently in a gigantic cavern, with a stony ceiling high above. They were standing on a cliff with the lava river snaking its way along a valley about a hundred feet deep and fifty feet across. Ruthard was leading them to a thin wooden bridge, stretched across the valley. Henry and Frank were dragged out onto this bridge.

"Now," said Ruthard, "I think this is an appropriate place for you to meet your end. I will kill the more talkative one first."

Henry was thrown on his back in front of Ruthard, who placed one foot firmly on his chest. Ruthard drew a sword out of his cloak, and held it above Henry's head. An electric glow emitted from the edge of the blade.

"Now, fiend," said Ruthard. "What is your name, that I may know who almost defeated me?"

Henry thought back to his old conversations with Frank in their dreary cell. He thought of the late night stories Frank would tell him. At last he said, "I am Henry, Henry Bolte!"

With this, Henry slipped the small laser out of his sleeve, and shot Ruthard's outstretched arm. Ruthard yelled in pain, dropping the energy sword, and collapsing in a heap next to Henry. Henry quickly jumped up, and grabbed Frank's large laser, which had been set on the ground nearby. He aimed at all the cloakies standing on the cliff, and was about to shoot them, when Ruthard kicked him from behind. Henry accidentally dropped the laser, causing it to slice through the bridge.

The two halves of the bridge swung downwards towards the sides of the valley. Though he did drop the large laser, Henry was able to grab onto the side of the bridge and prevent himself from falling, but he watched in horror as Frank swung to the other side.

Some of the cloakies grabbed onto the sides of the bridge, but most of them stumbled causing everyone to fall except the young man. He had been further behind everyone, and did not get caught in the jumble.

"Frank, no!!!" cried Henry in agony, as he watched his friend and all the cloakies fall towards the lava. Henry's sadness was interrupted when Ruthard kicked his hand. Ruthard had also held onto the edge of the bridge and he was just above Henry.

"Now you will join your friend," said Ruthard, kicking Henry's hand again, causing Henry to fall down a little lower, near the end of the bridge. "Go, Sandy! Go on without me!" he shouted to the young man, who had just reached the opposite cliff. The young man turned and ran off out of sight. Ruthard tried to reach a little farther downward, and kick Henry again, but he was now using his injured arm. He let out a yell of pain. Ruthard clutched his wounded arm, but this act caused him to go off balance, and he fell off the side of the bridge hurtling past Henry toward his fiery demise. Henry hung there until he mustered the strength to climb back onto the cliff, and he quietly wept there for some time, mourning the loss of Frank.

About a week after the overthrow of Amethyst Gorge, Henry sat in the upper rooms of one of the buildings. The other newly freed residents of Amethyst Gorge had elected him as their leader. Henry had immediately decided that they would summon agents from the New

Government to ensure the Amethyst Gorge would no longer be a den of slaveholders and warlords.

He was now working on a design for his tiny laser. He had kept it and treasured it, as it was his only physical memory of Frank. He was attempting to attach the laser to his mining helmet. Henry looked up from his work as a person entered the room. "Governor Bolte," he said. "We found an underground prison cell last night, and the people we released wish to see you."

"Show them in," said Henry. Henry's face lightened up when Fousel stepped into the room.

"Fousel," said Henry.

"Henry," said Fousel. The two friends embraced.

"We did it," said Henry, through his tears of joy.

"I know," said Fousel. "But I didn't know your last name was Bolte. I thought you didn't know what your last name was."

"It wasn't, but I am keeping the name in honor of Frank. He didn't make it, but let's not talk of that. Now we can find Mr. Fac again."

The two were interrupted when an old couple entered the room. "Hello, Governor Bolte," said the old man. "You have finally succeeded in bringing down that evil Ruthard. We tried to long ago, but we were unsuccessful, and he said death was too good for us."

"I used to have a little son," said his wife. "He should be a grown adult by now, but the thought of him has been a comfort to us, and we hope we will be able to find him again. His name was Henry."

"Where did you leave him?" asked Henry, beginning to feel joy and sadness rising through himself.

"We used to live on an island planet called Marentus..." the old man trailed off upon seeing the emotion in Henry's face.

"My name is Henry," said Henry, pushing back his tears, "and my parents left me on Marentus when I was very young. I never knew what happened to them." Henry rushed into the arms of his parents and the scene of joy and happiness that followed can hardly be described with words. Fousel and the resident who had brought him to the room stepped out. They waited some time, and Henry eventually came out. He looked like a new man, with all of his burdens removed.

Just then, another person came into the hallway. "Governor Bolte," he said, "A person has come who wants to see you." Henry was led along to the main hall, where the messenger opened the door for Henry, and then closed it behind him.

A figure was standing there amongst the overturned chairs and tables. She stepped forward into the light. "Hello, Henry," she said. "I am Magnesia Starbrand."

"Magnesia Starbrand!" said Henry, in astonishment. "Aren't you the head of the New Government?"

"I am," said Magnesia Starbrand.

"Why did you come?" asked Henry.

"This government I am leading," said Magnesia Starbrand. "is, as you said, very new. The area that it now controls is far too vast, for its novelty and scantiness, as is evident by the existence of such a place like this. Amethyst Gorge is a remarkable facility. Its obscurity, security, and defensibility make it an ideal location for defense. I have come, in part, to ensure that we have a firm foot in this location, as we can use it to extend law and order throughout the entire Grellion System. The New Government has need of places like this, but the New Government also has need of people. There are many like Ruthard Scott in this galaxy, men who rob and enslave others to secure their own prosperity. It is people like him that we are trying to find and root out, but they are hidden well. Worse, a new threat is rising that could unite them together. This facility is on a completely barren and uninhabitable planet, and we might never have found it but for your contacting us. You, Henry, have shown excellent abilities of courage and leadership. There are not many brave and resourceful people in the world, but it is only people who have these qualities that disrupt the plans of the selfish and evil. The New Government needs people like these, like you, Henry. The objective of my visit here is to invite you to join me. Will you join my military force and help bring peace to the galaxy?" Magnesia

Starbrand reached out her hand for Henry to shake. Henry considered for a moment, and then shook it.

"It's nice to meet you, Magnesia Starbrand," he said.

The Case of the Missing Gold

BY TROY MALIN

Jerry swung his pickax at the rocks. He wondered if there was gold in this plot of land. He considered what it would be like to be rich. He would probably settle down on a big ranch and raise a family.

"Hey Jerry, stop daydreaming and continue digging. I'm sure there is gold here just waiting for us to find it." It was Jerry's friend, Danny. They often worked together. One could never mistake Danny for someone else. He always wore a big, wide, broad brimmed brown hat to keep the sun off.

"Of course, Danny," replied Jerry. They dug into the ground with their pickaxes for a while.

"Hey, what's this?" exclaimed Jerry.

"What is it," asked Danny? Jerry turned over a pile of earth. They saw a glint.

"It looks like gold," said Jerry.

"By my hat," exclaimed Danny! "It is gold. You did it Jerry, old pal. You found our gold! We are going to be rich, rich, rich!" They quickly dug deeper. They found more gold. They had certainly struck it rich!

"What should we do with it," asked Jerry?

"I know of a secret cave where we can keep it safe," said Danny. "I discovered it yesterday. No one knows the place but me." Danny led Jerry past some big rocks and bushes.

"In here," said Danny. He pointed underneath a big rock. There didn't seem to be anything there. Jerry could not find it.

"I don't know where it is," he said.

"It's over here," said Danny. He led Jerry around a big bulging rock. There it was, a small cave only about 8 feet in depth.

"If we put the gold in here, no one will find it," said Danny. "It will be snug as a bug."

"Nice place," said Jerry. "No one will find it here."

"You said it," replied Danny. As Danny said this, he thought he heard some rocks falling. "It's probably nothing," thought Danny.

It took some time to load all the gold into the hole. It was heavy. They also had to transport it at night so no one saw them hauling piles of gold. Things might have gone sour, but at last it was done.

That night, Danny and Jerry were wondering what they would do next. Jerry wanted to settle down and live a peaceful life, but Danny wanted a life of adventure. He wanted to join the army with Jerry. So, they were at odds, but all that would change the next day.

Jerry was walking in the brisk morning and decided to check on their treasure. He went to the place and rounded the rock. The gold was gone! Jerry could not believe his eyes. How could it be so? He entered the cave in utter disbelief. Then he noticed something. There was a piece of paper on the floor. He picked it up. There was a note written on it. This is what it said:

Warning: Do not try to find your lost gold, or it will be the death of you. Signed, The Pickaxe.

Jerry ran all the way back to the camp.

"Danny, Danny," he cried. "The gold it's, it's gone!"

"By my hat, what do you mean," asked Danny? "How could the gold be gone? We put it in a safe place."

"I don't know," said Jerry. "This is quite a mystery."

"Oh good," said Danny. "I like good mysteries. Where do we start?"

"I better show you this," said Jerry. He held up the note.

"What's that," asked Danny?

"It is a notice," answered Jerry. "The thief left it." Danny took it up in his hand. He read it.

"The Pickaxe? Who is that?"

"I don't know," answered Jerry. "We better start looking for him and our gold."

"Well then," said Danny. "What are we waiting for? Let's go catch this thief." They both ran back to the cave.

"The first thing to do," said Danny, "is to look for clues. Let's search the cave." They both searched the cave. They found nothing except a message drawn on the wall.

Warning: Do not try to find your lost gold, or it will be the death of you. Signed, The Pickaxe

"There it is again," said Jerry. "I wonder when the thief will fulfill his nasty promise." Just then they both heard a rumble. It grew louder. Small rocks began to fall from the entrance. Then larger pieces began to fall. Before Danny and Jerry knew what had happened, the entrance was blocked up with rocks and stones.

"This must be a trap," exclaimed Jerry! "We have played right into the Pickaxe's hand!"

"This thief is certainly smart," said Danny. "He knew exactly what we would do."

"That's for sure," said Jerry. "We have been outsmarted this time." They then realized how dark it was. You couldn't see your hand in front of your face.

"How do we get out of here," wondered Jerry?

"Beats me," said Danny.

"Maybe we could find another exit," said Jerry.

"I don't believe that is possible," said Danny. "I looked this place over when I discovered it. I could not find any other way out."

"Let's search anyway," said Jerry. "It will give us something to do." They both groped around, feeling for an exit, but to no avail.

"What are we going to do," asked Jerry?

"I don't know," answered Danny. All of a sudden he tripped over a rock. "Oof," groaned Danny.

"Are you all right," asked Jerry, in a concerned voice?

"I think so," said Danny. Just then they heard a cracking noise. The floor beneath Danny and Jerry gave way and they both fell down, down, down into the darkness. They fell for a while, then they began to slide. The ground apparently was sloping steeply. Danny and Jerry slid for a while and then came to a stop.

"By my hat," exclaimed Danny! "That was awesome!"

"Sure, if you don't count the bruises," answered Jerry. "Ouch, it had to be on my sore arm."

"I say," said Danny. "There is something shiny ahead." There was, and as they approached it, Jerry let out a whoop for joy.

"Why, what do you know?" he said. "It's our gold!" It was. All their gold was piled up in a heap, and some daylight came from an opening up ahead. Then they both noticed something. There was a large picture of a pickaxe painted on the wall.

"I wonder what that pickaxe means," said Jerry. Just then the entrance to the cave darkened. Someone was coming. They heard a voice.

"I am The Pickaxe, and you are lucky you are still alive, but your luck has just run out. Prepare to die." As he said this, The Pickaxe drew out a torch and a laser lamp (a metal staff with electricity crackling from the top).

"Quick, back up the passage," cried Jerry! As they both ran back, they heard a noise like two poles being snapped together. Then they heard a noise like a flame thrower. A long laser beam shot out in front of them. The roof came down blocking their path.

"There is no escape," said the Pickaxe. "You will die". They looked back. They saw that the strange man had connected the laser lamp and the torch together, which seemed to increase the power of both.

"So that is where the laser beam came from," thought Jerry. "The laser lamp supercharges the torch, causing it to shoot out a laser." The Pickaxe had disconnected his two weapons, and charged at them.

"Quick," said Jerry! "Use the fallen rocks!" The two of them picked up rocks and began throwing them at the villain, but he just blocked them with his weapons. He had just reached them. He swung his laser lamp at Jerry who blocked it with a rock. Then The Pickaxe let out a cry, and dropped his laser lamp. His hand was hit by a rock Danny had thrown.

"Take that, you," said Danny! Then he picked up the laser lamp and swung it at the brigand. He blocked it with his torch. Then the two of them started a duel. It was fast and furious, but at last The Pickaxe burnt the laser lamp out of Danny's hand with his torch. It would have been the end of Danny if it had not been for Jerry, who anxiously watched the duel. When he saw Danny go down, he picked up a rock and threw it at The Pickaxe. It knocked the torch out of his hand. Then Danny picked up both weapons, and said to his opponent,

"Well I believe I have won. Surrender."

"Never," cried The Pickaxe! He ran to the mouth of the cave. Jerry and Danny followed. The cave ended abruptly at the edge of a cliff. The Pickaxe leapt off. Then a huge bird-like creature swooped down and caught him.

"We can't let him escape," said Jerry!

"And we won't," said Danny. For the first time in his life, Jerry saw Danny take off his hat. "I will stop him," said Danny. Then to Jerry's surprise, Danny flung his hat after the villain.

"Danny, what are you doing," asked Jerry, surprised?

"You will see," answered Danny. His hat flew toward The Pickaxe in record time. Soon it had caught up with him. It flew right into him. Knocking him off his flying steed. He fell down, down, down into the forest below.

"Nice move Danny," said Jerry.

"Thank you," replied Danny. Just then the creature reared round and they saw it was a pterodactyl. It was headed straight for them.

"Caw," it shrieked.

"Oh Dear," said Jerry. "I believe it is going to attack us." He ran back to the cave, but Danny remained where he was. He did not seem afraid. As the pterodactyl soared up, Danny stretched out his hand.

"Easy, boy, easy," said Danny. Then he placed his hand on the pterodactyl's beak. It calmed.

"Good boy. Good boy," said Danny. Then to Jerry's astonishment, Danny mounted on its back and flew around.

"Danny," shouted Jerry! "What are you doing!" Danny flew his pterodactyl down toward Jerry, and alighted in the cave's mouth.

"Can't you see I've made a new friend," said Danny?

"I do," answered Jerry, "but do you really mean to keep him?"

"Of course, I do," said Danny. "He is my new friend, and I also intend to keep these weapons. I have grown quite fond of them." Jerry saw that there was no point in resisting, so he agreed.

"Come on, let's go back to camp," said Danny. "Come on, Jerry. Get on"

"Are you sure," asked Jerry, hesitantly?

"I suppose you have a better idea," said Danny?

"Oh, all right," said Jerry. He reluctantly got on, and they both flew back to camp. It was later that night when Danny and Jerry heard a rustling.

"What's that," said Jerry?

"I don't know," said Danny, "Be on alert," They saw a figure moving towards them. Danny switched on his torch.

"Who goes there," he said?

"A friend," came the voice. Then a woman stepped into the light.

"Danny Bighat and Jerry Wilkans," she said, "I am Magnesia Starbrand, and I need your help with something that is of the utmost importance."

Ravens' Rise and Falcons' Fall

BY ZIMRY OSBURN

This is a tale of mourning; a tale of weeping; a tale of depression; a tale of loneliness. But this is also a tale of courage; a tale of bravery; but most of all, this is a tale of the rise of a hero. I am Bobby Net. This is my story.

Twang Bobby Net looked up from the sights of his crossbow. "Yes!"

All his training as a teen had really paid off. Jacob, his pet falcon, left his perch on Bobby's shoulder to fetch the crow Bobby had hit with an arrow. Up here in the mountains, hunting was his only means of surviving. As Jacob flew back overhead, Bobby realized that the bird he had hit wasn't a crow, it was a pigeon. Not only that, but the bird had a piece of paper wrapped around its leg!

"I've heard of this. It's called a carrier pigeon. I wonder what the message is?" He took the paper off the pigeon's leg and read it.

That Bobby Net is hunting too close to home base for comfort. Kill him.
– *The Raven*

Bobby Net didn't know why he was targeted. He didn't know who The Raven was. He only knew one thing. It was time to run! He whistled to Jacob, who then began to circle high in the sky. Bobby Net began running toward the forest. Jacob followed him from a distance. Bobby entered the forest. He looked around and listened for any signs of life. Nothing.

"That's odd." He thought.

Then, he smelled it, the unmistakable scent of smoke. Suddenly the voice of Smokey the Bear from an old commercial began echoing in his mind. "Forest fire. Forest fire. Forest fire." He realized why. The forest was on fire!

Bobby Net could only think of two things then: his house, and his horse, Cloudy, in his barn. He charged through the woods, now flaming, and dodged falling fiery branches and trees toppling from all the heat. He reached the outer hedge wall of his home, only to find it blazing and flaming. He ran to the entrance and found the ground was charred. He hesitated for a moment, then charged through, only to halt in horror at what he saw.

His house and barn were burnt to the ground. Bobby Net ran to the barn and to where Cloudy's stall used to be. All that was left of Cloudy was a pile of charred bones.

"No!"

Bobby had grown a close kinship to Cloudy. Maybe because he had nursed Cloudy's cuts from a thornbush, or maybe because they were both loners. But now he was dead. All Bobby had left were his crossbow and Jacob, who alighted on his shoulder. He reached up and stroked the bird's feathers. He shuffled over to his house to search for remains.

All that was left of his house was a single chair. Bobby studied it carefully. Carved into the wooden seat was a design. Bobby stood, shocked. The image looked like cursive capital T and R with wings and a beak! "The Raven?! Could it be?!"

Suddenly, Bobby heard a rustling in the forest. He snapped to attention. Another rustling! Bobby reached for his crossbow. A deer burst out of the woods. He relaxed. Then, he heard the sound of footsteps crunching on leaves. He ran. He didn't care who it was. He just ran. The crackling grew louder. A gruff voice called,

"There he goes! Get him!"

Bobby Net ran through the forest faster than he had ever run before. All his nervous energy fueled his speed. He made the edge of the forest in record time, bursting out onto the grassy plain. As he ran, he looked up and saw Jacob hovering overhead. It was a deadly mistake. He suddenly stumbled and tripped over a root. He flipped himself over, only to see someone fifty feet away pointing a gun at him.

"Stand up slowly," the man said, "or I'll shoot you right there." Bobby Net stood, eyeing the gunman carefully. "Now, take your medicine and die!"

At this moment, time seemed to slow down. The man aimed the gun. Jacob swooped out of nowhere, into the line of fire. The man pulled the trigger. Jacob clawed the barrel of the gun. The bullet hit Jacob. The man fired again. The bullet became stuck in the barrel and exploded, shredding the gun into hundreds of pieces. Jacob faltered, dropping to the ground in a pool of blood, dead.

"No!" Bobby Net cried. "Not you too!!" Then, Bobby felt a cloth slide over his mouth and nose. Everything went black.

Bobby Net came to his senses. His wrists were bound behind his back. He was on a cliffside. He looked down and saw a five-hundred-foot drop. He looked around. A man in a black wingsuit stood in front of Bobby, watching him.

"So, you're awake at last." Bobby shot a quick glance at his wrists, then stiffened at what he saw. Dynamite was tied to the ropes!

"Aughh!"

"In case you're wondering," the man in the wingsuit said. "Those are set to go off in ten minutes, and I plan to make like a tree and leave before that happens. But first, let me show you something."

He pulled a strange contraption from the ground and held it up. It was a yellow box with one side open, attached to a metal pole, with a black wiry mesh-like cloth sticking partway out of the hole.

"This is a net shooter. It was your grandfather's. I took it from him when I killed him and his squadron during Nexar War."

"What!" exclaimed Bobby. "You, you murderer!" Bobby Net strained at his bonds but to no avail. The man in the wingsuit slapped him across the face.

"Shut up!" The man regained a calm composure. "Now, as I was saying, I've decided it's time to end you and your family line once and for all. As we speak, a missile is being aimed at your parents' home, right down there." He pointed over the edge of the cliff. Down at the bottom of the cliff, was the biggest missile Bobby had ever seen. "A bit overkill, isn't it?" The Raven asked, for that truly was his identity. "Either way, it'll do," he said.

Bobby thought for a moment about his is poor parents. He couldn't let this happen! He took a second to gather his strength, and without warning, he kicked The Raven in the gut. He rolled over and for reasons beyond his understanding, grabbed the net shooter, and then continued rolling off the cliff.

Bobby Net knew he would definitely die from the impact on hitting the ground. But he also knew that if he could land on the missile, both the dynamite and the missile itself would explode, preventing them from firing it at his parents' house. But, he would still die. He was glad to die heroically, like Jacob, but he wished it didn't have to end like this. He could see the ground.

Suddenly, a brilliant laser burst from the clouds, severing his bonds. Then, to Bobby's disbelief, a pterodactyl swooped down and snatched him out of the air. He looked down. The dynamite struck right on target, causing a brilliant ball of flames to rocket up. The pterodactyl opened its mouth and swooped toward the wreckage. A hand latched on to his wrist. He looked up. A man with a big brown hat reached down to help him up. They were upon the wreckage now. The pterodactyl opened its mouth and started sucking in all the fire. It swallowed. The man spoke.

"Bobby Net, I am Danny Bighat. You may not know this, but the galaxy is inhabited by an evil far greater than imaginable. I, on behalf of Magnesia Starbrand, ask you to join us in battle.

Maktuf: The Origin Story

BY DANIEL DE LA TORRIENTE

    This is the story of the Storm Commando, ARC-General Maktuf, and how he became one of Titan's most formidable accomplices.
    Maktuf grew up on the planet Rialta, in the Energy Dimension, where there are Shadow Monks that wield the Blades of Darkness, and characters called Storm Commandos, who are trained from a very young age in the art of war. But he wasn't exactly like the others. He had been entrusted with a Blade of Darkness by an old Shadow Monk who had past the year before while defending against all evils.
    An advanced and mysterious traveler had entered the Energy Dimension through a Versible Portal, giving the universe a way to access other dimensions. You see, when you activate a Versible Portal somewhere, it stays there for others to use, permanently. So, when this traveler had gone through, other unwanted visitors were able to just walk right in. Then, one day.... one bad guy did just that.
    Maktuf was training in the facility he constructed for militaristic purposes on a new planet, Dayna, when he heard a noise coming from outside the blast shield doors. It sounded like shouting and footsteps coming his way quickly. "Someone could be in trouble," he thought to himself. He was about to open the doors, when he heard voices from outside.
    "Find that Storm Commander," said the voice. "My master wants him dead or alive." Then there were more footsteps. Then the noise was gone.

"I wonder what they wanted?" Maktuf thought to himself. He was the only Storm Commando he knew of on the whole planet. "Could they be hunting for me?" He had a bunch of questions. He decided to walk it off though. So, he set off for the park where he often went to think about things. It was a beautiful place. He was sitting underneath a tree when he heard a voice call out.

"It's him! Capture him." It was the same voice he had heard earlier. He looked around to find a man in a black suit pointing a Sword of Darkness at him. He also saw what looked like this mysterious person's henchmen coming towards him with an array of weapons. Some carried blades and axes, while others wielded laser cannons and flamethrowers.

"Oh, no!" he said, tripping over a branch as he turned to flee. He was a fast runner. Unfortunately so was the leader of the group. He flew past the henchmen in pursuit of his quarry.

"Get back here, in the name of the Rogue Allegiance!" he shouted.

"Where have I heard that name before?" Maktuf asked himself. He thought about it a bit too hard, and he ran smack into a giant oak tree and collapsed, knocked out.

Maktuf eventually came around to find himself in a dark room filled with what looked like a collection of paintings. He heard footsteps and then a figure entered the room. The light was turned on brighter and Maktuf was able to see his captor. He was wearing a black helmet and black garment that looked sewn onto his armor.

"Hello, again," the ominous figure said.

"If I wasn't tied up, I'd make that the last time you'll say that." Maktuf replied hatefully. The stranger laughed deviously.

"That's what they all say, until you get a feel for our superior power." With the flick of a switch, the lights illuminated the paintings and Maktuf stared at them with a horrified look in his eye. He looked closer and saw they weren't actually paintings, but photographs taken of fallen Shadow Monks, other Storm Commandos, and what looked like Reapers, which he had heard vague descriptions of from Storm Commandos that had seen them on other planets.

"This, this is what happens when you underestimate the Rogue Allegiance's might," Maktuf's captor said with pride.

"Why did you capture me?" Maktuf asked in an annoyed tone.

"Well, to put it simply, my master insisted that you are invaluable and must be obtained at all costs," the captor responded.

"And just who might be your master?" Maktuf inquired.

The captor laughed and said, "The Rogue." He laughed a little again, and then rudely left the room, with his footsteps fading away. But Maktuf didn't need any more information. He knew exactly who The Rogue was from what Storm Commandos had told him. Apparently, he had attacked his own planet and killed more than half his own kind.

"I'm in a pit now, aren't I?" he said to himself."

"Well, not really," a whisper came from above Maktuf. He looked up to find what looked like a Reaper staring at him with what might have been a friendly smile (well Maktuf would have seen a smile if the figure were not wearing a dark blue hood and mask). "Don't worry I'm here to rescue you." The stranger said with reassurance.

"Who are you?" Maktuf was in awe at the fact that his rescuer was hanging on the ceiling with nothing to hold onto, let alone, how he got into the cave base.

"I am Forum," said the figure, answering back. "How I'm here is not important right now, but I'm trying to get you out of here, so let's go." They hurried down the corridors, Forum led the way so they could escape as quickly as possible. They made it out of the secret base through an exit which was at a riverbed near the park.

"No wonder I heard noises around here." Maktuf said, chuckling.

"We're almost to the ship," Forum said. "By the way, what's your name?"

"I'm Maktuf, and because you saved me from harm, Forum, I will always have your back."

Epilogue

Magnesia Starbrand looked down over her map of the terrain on the planet Nessogis. Her scouts had already reported that a force was gathering on a high ground known as Table Hill. The fate of many of the people of this galaxy might be decided on that grassy knoll.

It had been but a few days ago when Magnesia had received a message from a strange group calling themselves the Rogue Allegiance, allied under a strange leader, called The Rogue, which declared the necessity of a change in government and demanded her presence on Table Hill.

She had long been aware that there were many here pursuing their own rise in power. It was no wonder that Purple-Hood had so easily agreed to surrender this part of the galaxy to her. During the past few years she had been hunting down all of the ex-aristocrats she could find, but she had always been aware that there were a great many still undiscovered. However, up until now, these barons had been easy enough to uproot, once they were found. Magnesia's only fear had been that they would unite into a single force capable of resisting her New Government's forces.

That fear had now come to pass. From what her scouts had reported, the force on Table Hill was greater than any she had encountered since the days of the Resistance to Purple-Hood. This force would take a lot more to subdue than any of the others. Magnesia only hoped that they would be able to defeat it before even more rebels and pirates were able to join it.

Even though this Rogue Allegiance was the true culmination of her worst fears, she was not without preparation. These past few years had also been a time of recruitment and gathering of force. She had found many soldiers, miners, and hunters living near and far, some from indeed very far. But, they all had the beginnings of heroes, and she would need many in the upcoming times.

"Commander Starbrand," said General Bighat, walking into the room. "The forces have been assembled and we are ready to depart for Table Hill."

"Good, let's head out," said Magnesia. She stood up and grabbed her broadsword. It was wrought of silver, and the hilt was studded with shining red diamonds. Magnesia had not needed to use it for some time, but something told her that she would use far more in the upcoming days than ever in her long, war-torn career.

The times that were coming would be difficult and dangerous. Many would not survive. These recruits had their hero beginnings, but war is the force that separates the feeble from the bold, the environment in which true heroes are made.

www.ingramcontent.com/pod-product-compliance
Lightning Source LLC
LaVergne TN
LVHW012036060526
838201LV00061B/4634